LEGO CITY

LOOK OUT BELOW!

By Michael Anthony Steele
Illustrated by Kenny Kiernan

SCHOLASTIC INC.

ISBN 978-0-545-41555-2

LEGO, the LEGO logo, the Brick and Knob configurations and the Minifigure are trademarks of the LEGO Group. © 2012 The LEGO Group. Produced by Scholastic Inc. under license from the LEGO Group.

18/0

40

18

Designed by Angela Jun
Printed in the U.S.A.
First printing, July 2012

Hoot!
The work whistle blows.
George and Johnny arrive at
the gold mine.

3

The trucks are filled with rocks.
The rocks have gold inside.

"Gold mining really rocks!"
Johnny cheers.

George and Johnny ride in a cart.
Everyone wears safety gear.

Rummmmble!
A drill digs the large tunnels.

"I really dig that drill," says Johnny.

George uses a jackhammer.
It breaks apart the large rocks.

The boulders are loaded onto a trailer.
"Let's rock and roll," says Johnny.

The trailer goes out of the tunnel.

The miners take a break. They eat sandwiches.

One miner reaches for a drink. He bumps into a lantern.

"Good thing we have our head lamps," says George.

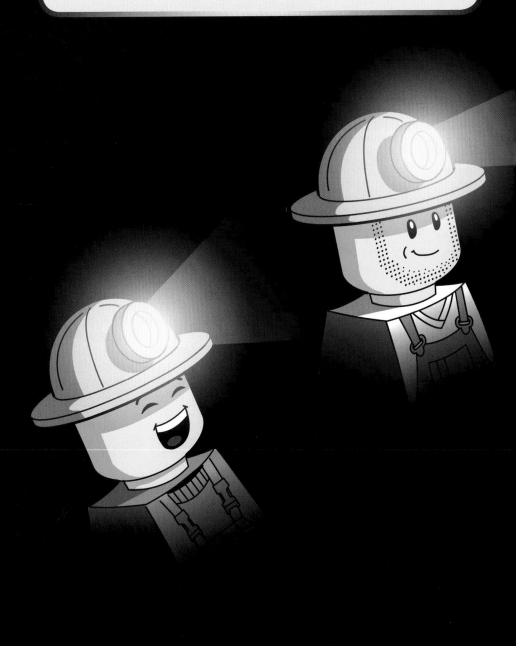

Johnny fixes the lamp.

He looks at the wall where the lamp fell.

There is gold in the rock.

George sets the timer.

Then everyone leaves the mine.

The dust settles.
Everyone returns to the mine.

"Look at all that gold," says George.

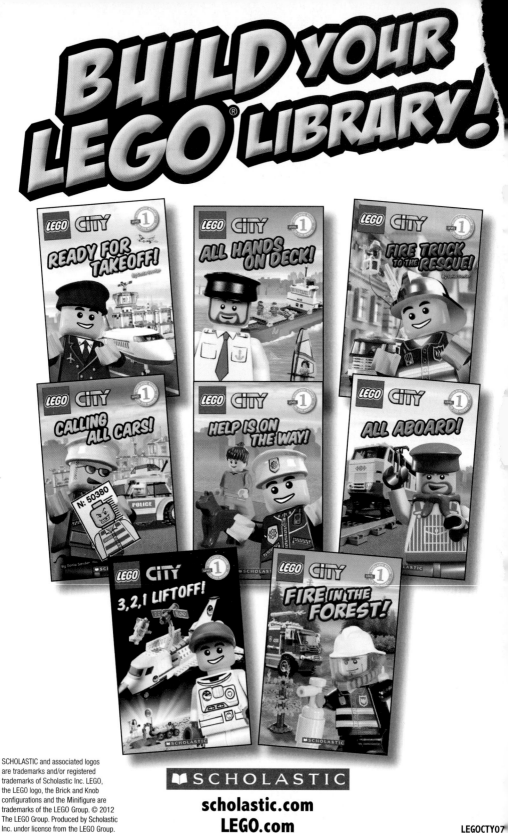

scholastic.com
LEGO.com

LEGOCTY07